To my mischievous siblings
who inspire me, and fuel my
wicked sense of humour.

First published 2017 by Two Hoots
This edition published 2018 by Two Hoots
an imprint of Pan Macmillan
20 New Wharf Road, London N1 9RR.
Associated companies throughout the world
www.panmacmillan.com
ISBN: 978-1-5098-4268-1
Text and illustrations © Bethan Woollvin 2017, 2018
Moral rights asserted.

1 3 5 7 9 8 6 4 2
A CIP catalogue record for this book is available from the British Library.
Printed in China
The illustrations in this book were painted in gouache on cartridge paper.

www.twohootsbooks.com

This **TWO HOOTS** book
belongs to

- - - - - - - - -

Bethan Woollvin

Rapunzel

TWO HOOTS

Rapunzel lived all alone in a tall, dark tower.

She was trapped there by a witch, who visited every day.

"Rapunzel, Rapunzel, let down your hair!" called the witch.
And then, using Rapunzel's hair as a rope, up she climbed,
because that was the only way in to the tower.

Every day, the witch brushed
Rapunzel's hair, swish, swish.

Then

Snip,

Snip

she stole some golden locks to sell for riches.

As she left with her treasure, the witch cackled,
"You can never escape, Rapunzel! Leave the tower,
and I will put a terrible curse on you!"

But was Rapunzel frightened? Oh no, not she!

If the witch could use her hair to get in,
Rapunzel could use it to get out.

So one day, she did.

After
climbing
down from
the tower,
Rapunzel pulled
her hair free,
and looked around.
Then she started
to explore.

The thought of returning
to the tower made her sad.
It's a shame about that witch,
she thought to herself.

So Rapunzel made a plan. She worked on it secretly every day.

And with the help of a new friend she had made from the forest, she was always safely back in the tower before the witch came.

The witch never suspected a thing.

Until one day . . .

"RAPUNZEL!"

The witch found a leaf in Rapunzel's hair.

But was Rapunzel frightened? Oh no, not she!
"The wind must have blown it in through
the window," she said boldly.

"Well remember," snarled the witch,
"If you ever leave the tower, I will put
a TERRIBLE curse on you."

And with that, she grabbed the end of Rapunzel's hair and climbed out of the window.

But the witch

didn't get far before

Snip, Snip,

she was sent

tumbling

to the ground.

The witch's cursing days were done.

So Rapunzel climbed out of the tower for the last time, down into the forest where her friend was waiting.

And were the other witches frightened?
Oh yes indeed!

FROM THE AUTHOR
Bethan Woollvin

The original tale of *Rapunzel* is about a
young lady who is saved from the enchantment of an
evil witch by a prince. This *Rapunzel,* however, has a bit
of a twist. My new version was inspired by all of my brothers
and sisters, who lend me their imaginations whenever I'm
creating new stories and characters. With this book, I wanted
to deliver to readers a braver, more resourceful Rapunzel,
who doesn't need to be saved by a prince.